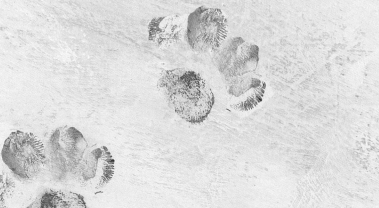

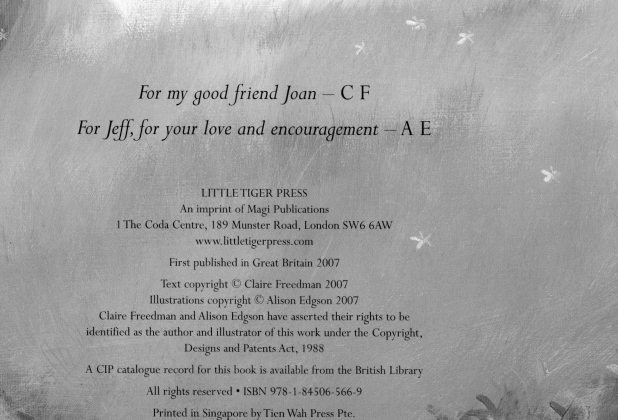

For my good friend Joan — C F

For Jeff, for your love and encouragement — A E

LITTLE TIGER PRESS
An imprint of Magi Publications
1 The Coda Centre, 189 Munster Road, London SW6 6AW
www.littletigerpress.com

First published in Great Britain 2007

A CIP catalogue record for this book is available from the British Library

Printed in Singapore by Tien Wah Press Pte.

2 4 6 8 10 9 7 5 3 1

Follow That Bear If You DARE!

Claire Freedman

illustrated by

Alison Edgson

LITTLE TIGER PRESS
London

Hare loved bears.
He liked big bears, little bears,
hairy bears and scary bears.
   "If only I could find a bear,"
said Hare. "If only I could catch one!
The hairier and scarier the better!"

So Hare bought a book: *The Best Book of Bear Hunting*. He opened his book and took a look.

"Podgy Rabbit!" called Hare. "I need you for a Very Important Bear Hunt!"

"A Bear Hunt?" said Podgy Rabbit. "How do you hunt for bears?"

"It's all in my book," explained Hare. So he turned the page, and they took a look.

STEP 2

THINGS YOU WILL NEED

TO catch your bear,

take a fishing net,

some string – as long as

you can get –

	L	S	D
~~	20	0	0
~~	10	5	2
~~	0	2	4
~~	30	7	6

A TORCH to shine
deep inside his lair,
and watchful eyes ~

BEARS LURK EVERYWHERE!

"Are you sure you want to find a bear, Hare?" said Podgy Rabbit.

"Of course!" Hare said. "The hairier and scarier the better! Look, I've found a fishing net, a torch and a piece of string. What's next?"

They turned another page in Hare's book and took a look.

STEP 3

TRAILING YOUR BEAR

Now bears are not always
easily found,
so look out for pawprints
on the ground.

Crouch down low but please beware –
THE BIGGER THE
PAWPRINT,
THE BIGGER THE
BEAR!

"I don't think I like the sound
of Bear Hunting," said Podgy Rabbit anxiously.
"I hope we don't find any bear prints!"
   "Over here!" called Hare excitedly. "I've
found some!"
   "Oh dear!" said Podgy Rabbit. "They must
belong to a VERY hairy, scary bear. Now what?"

They turned another page of Hare's
book and took a look.

STEP 4

WHAT TO LOOK OUT FOR

BEARS like to scratch on a favourite tree, it sharpens their claws quite nastily.

THEIR nails stay as sharp as the teeth in their jaws.

The deeper the scratch marks, the sharper the claws!

"I really don't like the idea
 of Bear Hunting!" cried Podgy Rabbit.
"Let's go back!"
    "Not now!" cried Hare excitedly. "We're
on the trail! And look what I've found!"
    Podgy Rabbit looked. "Oh no!" he cried.
"Now what do we do?"
    "I'll tell you," said Hare. "It's all in my book."

So they turned another page
and took a look.

Rumble
Grumble!

"Shh! Did you hear that?" whispered
Hare excitedly. "That sounds like a very
hungry bear to me!"

"Hear it," trembled Podgy Rabbit. "I was
almost deafened by it! Quick, Hare, let's
take another look in your book!"

STEP 6

MEETING YOUR BEAR

MEETING your bear
can be quite shocking,
don't let him see
your knees are knocking.

SUCK in your tummy
and try to look thinner,
and hope that he's already
eaten his dinner!

"Yikes!" gulped Podgy Rabbit. "Look
over there, Hare!"
"Where?"
"It's a BEAR!"

"HELP! We'll never catch HIM with a fishing net
and a piece of string!" trembled Podgy Rabbit.
"Just watch me try!" cried Hare.
"I'm HUNGRY!" growled the bear.
Then, suddenly...

"Dinner's ready," called Mummy Bear.

"It's bear-sized beans on bear-sized toast."

"Yummy!" said Little Bear. "Must go!"

"Come back!" called Hare.
Poor Podgy Rabbit was too weak to speak!
"Oh no," cried Hare. "I can't lose
my bear – that's not fair!"

Quickly he took another look in his book.

STEP 7

WHAT BEARS LIKE TO EAT

A HUNGRY bear with an appetite will eat up any food in sight.

And all bears hate baked beans on toast

But love ripe hares and rabbits the most!

Podgy Rabbit quickly grabbed
Hare's paw.
"Run for it, Hare! It's lucky those
bears have never read your book.
For if they did, I bet they'd try to make
a hare and rabbit pie!"